For Ally, Conor and Aidan —J. S.

Dedicated to the everlasting spirit of my friend
Scott Wendell —K. F.

This edition published by Chronicle Books LLC in 2005.

Text © 1995 by Joan Sweeney.
Illustrations © 1995 by Kathleen Fain.

Book design by Laura Jane Coats and Suellen Ehnebuske.
Typeset in Stempel Schneidler.
Manufactured in China.
ISBN 0-8118-5079-X

The Library of Congress cataloged the previous edition as follows:
Sweeney, Joan, 1930-
Once upon a lily pad / by Joan Sweeney; illustrated by Kathleen Fain.
28 p. 16.5 cm.
Summary: Hector and Henriette, the most famous frogs in France, befriend an old painter in a battered straw hat.
ISBN 0-8118-0868-8
[1. Monet, Claude. 1840-1926—Fiction. 2. Frogs—Fiction. 3. Artists—Fiction.] I. Fain, Kathleen, ill. II. Title.
PZ7.S97426On 1995 [E]—dc20 94-46655 CIP AC

Distributed in Canada by Raincoast Books
9050 Shaughnessy Street, Vancouver, British Columbia V6P 6E5

10 9 8 7 6 5 4 3 2 1

Chronicle Books LLC
85 Second Street, San Francisco, California 94105

www.chroniclekids.com

Once Upon a Lily Pad

FROGGY LOVE IN MONET'S GARDEN

by Joan Sweeney
illustrated by Kathleen Fain

chronicle books · san francisco

*O*n the day Hector and Henriette were married, the water garden never looked lovelier. All the water lilies were in bloom. The groom was a handsome tenor whose splendid voice filled the air with song. His bride was the most sought-after beauty in all of France.

Everyone came to the wedding – from the tiniest tadpole to the biggest bullfrog. They gathered beneath the Japanese bridge and heard the sacred words: "I now pronounce you frog and wife."

They were all having
such a marvelous time
they scarcely noticed two
uninvited guests.

One was an old painter
in a battered straw hat.
The other was Monsieur
Crow, keeping a sharp eye
on the festivities from his
perch high above.

The newlyweds took up residence in the most fashionable corner of the pond. There they lazed away the hours, floating about and dining on dragonflies. So it was some while before they finally noticed the old painter.

He arrived every morning and quickly went to work. Soon
Hector and Henriette were convinced he was painting their
portraits. After all, weren't they the most celebrated frogs in
all of France? And so they graciously posed.

*H*ector and Henriette posed for the painter at sunrise, when the early morning mists veiled the pond. They posed in the brilliant light of noon. And they posed in the violet shadows of evening. The old man never seemed to tire of his work. But before long, Hector and Henriette began to tire of theirs.

"All this posing is a bore," Henriette complained.

"It's not easy being famous," Hector agreed.

High above, Monsieur Crow was listening.

"The old man is not painting you!" he cawed. "He's painting *me*!"

Hector and Henriette could not believe it. Who would want a portrait of a crow?

*F*ortunately, they soon had more important things to think about. They became the proud parents of tadpoles. The old man was enchanted. Not a day went by that he didn't paint the whole family frolicking among the lily pads.

"So there, Monsieur Crow!" laughed Hector and Henriette. But Monsieur Crow had other ideas.

One day he swooped down and began snapping up tadpoles in his sharp pointed bill.

"Stop!" cried Hector and Henriette. "Stop this minute, you nasty old crow!"

All at once the old painter sent a stone flying across the pond. It struck Monsieur Crow in the wing. Monsieur Crow was so insulted, he flew off in a snit and never came back again.

But the old painter came back day after day. And from then
on, Hector and Henriette always posed happily. The tadpoles
grew into frogs. Soon the chill air turned the leaves gold.
Hector and Henriette snuggled up in a comfortable cranny.

They hoped the old man would find a cozy place too.

The next spring, they were pleased to find him back at his easel. Before long, another family of tadpoles arrived. So it went, year after year.

Then one spring, the old painter did not appear. Hector and Henriette sat on their lily pad, watching for his familiar straw hat. When summer arrived and he had not returned, they knew that he would never be back.

That was long ago. In the years that followed, Hector and Henriette told their children and their children's children how, once upon a lily pad, the most famous frogs in all of France posed for an old painter in a battered straw hat.

It is said he was painting the water lilies during those years at the pond. But if you look very closely, down among the lily pads, it's possible you will find Hector and Henriette.

One thing is certain.
You will never find Monsieur Crow.

This is how the artist signed his name.